o o k s

Riverhead B
New Yor
1997

SOUL KISS

a novel

Shay Youngblood

Riverhead Books
a division of G. P. Putnam's Sons
Publishers Since 1838
200 Madison Avenue
New York, NY 10016

Published simultaneously in Canada

Library of Congress Cataloging-in-Publication Data

Youngblood, Shay.
Soul kiss: a novel/by Shay Youngblood.
p. cm.
ISBN 1-57322-063-9 (acid-free paper)
1. Afro-American families—Georgia—Fiction.
2. Afro-American women—Georgia—Fiction.
3. Afro-Americans—Georgia—Fiction.
I. Title.
PS3575.O8685S68 1997 96-51142 CIP
813'.54—dc21

Printed in the United States of America
1 3 5 7 9 10 8 6 4 2

This book is printed on acid-free paper. ∞

BOOK DESIGN AND PHOTOS
BY JUDITH STAGNITTO ABBATE

for Laura & my father

NO LONGER THE PROPERTY OF
BALDWIN PUBLIC LIBRARY

SOUL KISS

ONE